Clyde and I Help a Hippo to Fly

Written by **Russ Towne**

Illustrated by **Josh McGill**

Clyde and I slurped burzleberry tea

as we laid in the shade of a tickletoe tree

Its feathery leaves swayed in the breeze

tickling my toes and Clyde's knobby knees.

We giggled and laughed like best friends do,

rolled on the grass and blew bubbles, too.

What we saw next made us feel bad:

A hippo walked by looking real sad.

"Hi. I'm Marty McDinkle, and my friend here is Clyde."

"Hi. I'm Avianna," the hippo replied.

On her face was the trace of a tear.

Clyde asked, "What is the matter my dear?"

"I see you've been crying," Clyde softly said.

"May I ask what is wrong? Your eyes are
   all red."

So Avianna sat and told her sad tale.

"I dream of flying but I always fail.

And what makes it even harder

is I'm not fond of being in water.

So all the hippos make fun of me;

they say I'm not the way I'm supposed to be.

Then they sing a mean old song

And sing and sing it all day long:

"Splishetty, splashetty

Dippity dashetty

What kind of hippo are you?

We all love the water and you should, too.

Everyone knows hippos can't fly

So get your big head out of the sky;

Come down in the mud with us

And stop making such a fuss!

Splishetty, splashetty

Dippity dashetty

What kind of hippo are you?

We all love the water and you should, too."

Clyde said, "What an awful thing they do,
to sing that unkind song to you."

Avianna added, "Then the birds heard,
and made a song,

They chirp and chortle it all day long:"

"Quaketty Honketty
Squawketty Coo

Your featherless dream will never come true.

Why even try? You'll just get hurt.

Stay safe down there in the dirt.

Quacketty Honketty Squawketty Coo

Your featherless dream will never come true."

Avianna cried, "Nothing is going to keep me down;

I belong in the sky not on the ground.

So I tried real hard to build some wings

made of feathers, wood, and strings.

I jumped from the top of a hill nearby

And, for a moment, I was in the sky;

Then my wings broke and I thought I'd crash,

But I hit the lake with a great big splash.

I then bought a ticket for an airplane ride

And walked up the ramp to the plane
with pride,

But when I squeezed in the narrow door

All of a sudden I crashed through the floor.

Hippo-sized tears fell from her eyes.

But Clyde said, "You're in for a big surprise.

I know how you'll fly real soon

We'll build you a big hot air balloon.

We all got busy and worked as a team

so our new friend could live her dream.

Building the balloon was so much fun,

before we knew it we were done.

Clyde and I were filled with pride

when Avianna climbed inside

Clyde cranked the burner way up high;

and soon the balloon was in the sky.

But… The basket and we were still
on the ground!

That's when we heard a frightful sound.

The ropes started to squeak, shiver,
and groan

and the basket began to creak, quiver,
and moan.

All that noise gave us quite a big scare,

then all of a sudden we were in the air!

Clyde and I cheered, "Hippo, Hippo, Hooray!

Avianna Hippo you've made our day!"

She blushed and smiled as we flew.

Clyde told her, "It's all because of you.

You had a dream you wouldn't let die,

and thanks to it, we ALL can fly!

A bloat of hippos in the water below

Saw her fly by with her face all aglow.

Shocked flocks of birds flying quite high

were amazed to see Avianna fly by.

"Dear friends," she yelled, "my dream came true,

and I believe it can happen for you;

dare to dream big and do all you can.

I'll cheer you on and be a big fan.

The world needs dreamers who are doers, too,

And always remember I'm rooting for you!"

THE END

DEDICATION

To my family and friends. I'm blessed and grateful to have you in my life.

ACKNOWLEDGEMENTS

Special thanks to:

My wife Heidi for hanging in there through thick and thin, and for your expert and patient feedback regarding my ideas for children's books.

Ian and Susan Stevens for always being there when it means the most.

Bob and Jane Fukuda for your generosity.

Ute Lark for answering the call and being such an enthusiastic supporter and friend.

Josh McGill for being such a great illustrator, and for being easy to work with, patient, helpful, professional, someone who keeps his word, and meets deadlines.

Polly Letofsky for your advice, encouragement, and information regarding book publishing.

Karen M. Smith from Hen House Publishing for her excellent and fast editing services.

Sam Hurst Wallis of Sam Wallis Design + Illustration for her partial re-design for this second edition.

ACKNOWLEDGEMENTS CONTINUED

When I called for help, they answered. These are many of the people who helped me to launch my first children's books. They're listed in the approximate chronological order in which I received their support:

Bob and Jane Fukuda

Sue Stevens

Larson Rider

Tom Feasby

Paul Kinzelman

Joe Sabolefski

Brad Peppard

Ute Lark

Annette and George L'Italien

Steve Cross

Moe Rubenzahl

Roth Herrlinger

Keith Britany

Denis Loiseau

Michael Tarens

Pat Diamond

Tony Christopher

Alan Quinonez

Kim Miller

Mike Weston

Brian and Kristi Towne

Doug Greig

Glenn Fraser

John Nadler

Stefan Schmitz

Scott Schroeder

Francis DaCosta

Ken Cahill

Ted and June Okano

Diane Rawn

Patrick Morin

Ken K.

Ben and Erika Towne

Jerry Raitzer

Les and Denise Harris

Jay Larrick

Some other people also backed me, but requested their names not be mentioned on this list.

To all who supported me: I'm forever grateful for your help in bringing these books to life in the hands of young children and the young-at-heart.

THANK YOU for helping to me to begin my great adventure as an author and publisher of about thirty books in less than five years.